Two Knocks For Arthur

Daz Eek

Note From Author

Please note, as an English author, it's only natural for me to use UK spellings rather than those of American English, like 'colour' instead of 'color', for example. I hope you enjoy the story!

> Join Daz Eek's newsletter for news on future book releases at https://dazeek.blog/.

Contents

Morning

Arthur Underwood's return home from work had been without drama, but drama—small, medium, or large—had a way of calling on Arthur in the same way annoying Uncle Reg or Auntie Jean is, eventually, odds on to come calling for other people. The day on the calendar for their arrival may be unknown, but the eventuality of their knocking on the door, knock knock, was as certain as bills being shoved through the letterbox. So it was that Arthur trudged up the gravel driveway to a large mock-Tudor house as the lampposts were retiring from their nightly duty, with drama found and put away in his backpack along with his empty thermos and sandwich box. Drama to come calling. Drama to come knocking, knock knock. Oh, poor Arthur.

Arthur had only moved to his new digs three weeks ago, and so it still felt strange to him returning to the house, as though perhaps he'd taken a wrong turn along the way and was now trespassing with a threat of being chased off the premises by a large and gnashing dog. It was an overall sense of jarring newness that would move with him from the outside of the house to its insides, often fixing upon his face an expression of discomfort when he'd have to, for instance, leave his bedsit to go down a flight of stairs to visit the bathroom, or an expression of alarm when one of the other tenants, who occupied other bedsits down and up the house, would rattle their doors, forcing him to hurry away so he wouldn't have to let on that he now lived in the house too and wasn't really the murderer prowling the shadows of the house for his next victim, as yesterday's Birmingham Mail might suggest. The newspaper's headline, for which the typesetter had, no doubt gleefully, used the biggest and blackest font available, read: **BRUTAL MURDERER BAFFLES POLICE.** Arthur knew that as a man prone to various and crushing bouts of worry, he shouldn't have picked up the newspaper left behind on the empty seat next to him on his bus ride home. He certainly shouldn't have read the lurid, front-page story. Rather, it would've been best if he'd stuck to the safety, for him at least, of the sports back pages, reading for a second time instead of the latest on Aston Villa's transfer interest in a Brazilian defensive midfielder.

Arthur thought of the newspaper stuffed inside of his backpack. It suddenly felt as though he'd brought the murderer and their many victims back home with him. Why on earth hadn't he left the newspaper on the bus where he'd found it? Why did he do such things to himself? A hot panic overtook him, prickling his skin to a sweaty itch. There was nothing else for it. He'd have to promptly free himself of the newspaper. He couldn't live with a written reference to the atrocities inside of the bedsit with him, even ripped up into a thousand pieces and thrown into the bin. What if, when disposing of eggshells, he inadvertently caught sight of the corner of a letter 'M'? 'M' stood for **MURDERER**. What nightmares would come of it!

Arthur hurried towards six metal dustbins lined up in a neat row outside of the house: one allotted to him, with the remaining dustbins for the house's four other tenants living on the house's first and second floors, and the owners of the house, two elderly sisters, who occupied the house's expansive ground floor. At his dustbin, labelled conveniently with his name, he removed his backpack, unzipped it, and pulled out the newspaper. As he was lifting the dustbin lid and about to drop the newspaper inside of the bin, he heard the shout: "Don't do that!" As if caught doing something he shouldn't have been doing, Arthur dropped the dustbin lid to the ground, where it clattered and wobbled about before it eventually rested noiseless and still about his shoes. He turned to see Ethel, one of his landlords and five feet worth of bones and wool, shuffling towards him with arms outstretched, wrinkly fingers wriggling in a way that communicated she wanted something from him.

"Is that yesterday's?" Ethel asked.

With more sloppiness than sleight of hand, Arthur hid the newspaper behind his back. "Pardon?"

"I saw you from the kitchen window. The newspaper. Is it yesterday's?"

"Newspaper?"

"The one you're hiding behind your back."

Discovered, Arthur brought the newspaper out into the open. "This newspaper?"

"Do you have another behind your back?"

"No."

"Then that's the paper I'm talking about. Is it yesterday's?"

Arthur looked down at the newspaper as though the date of its publication was a complete mystery, *umming* and *ahhing* to himself as he attempted to buy time for the absolute right thing to say. His landlord couldn't have the newspaper. "It's today's, I think," he said.

"You think?" Ethel asked.

"I'm not sure."

"Not sure?"

"No, I'm sure. It's definitely today's."

Ethel read what she could see of the newspaper. "There's nothing about 'baffled police' in today's headline. Today's is all about the heads."

"Are you sure?" Arthur asked, as the horror of the news story once again tumbled front and centre into his consciousness.

"Do I look simple? We have the paper delivered every day, and I don't forget my headlines. I don't even forget the classifieds. You never know what you might read in the classifieds that's worth knowing. Now there's a tip for you."

Arthur saw a way out for himself. "You must've read yesterday's if you have the paper delivered every day."

"Our Mildred burnt it." Ethel said. "They'd all sold out by the time I went looking for a replacement."

"Burnt it?"

"That's my sister for you."

The last thing Arthur wanted to do was to prolong the conversation, but he knew he wouldn't be able to sleep thinking that one of his two landlords possessed arsonist tendencies. "Why would she burn your newspaper?" he asked.

"One of her spells," Ethel said. "And what of you? Isn't throwing away a perfectly good and unread-to-some newspaper the same as burning it? Or did I catch you casting a spell, too?"

"Spell, as in magic spell?"

"That would be it."

"Good grief, no. I know nothing about spells."

"Are you certain about that? Looked to me like you were trying to rid yourself of something. Not just the paper, mind you. My Mildred, she was trying to rid us all of something, too. She doesn't think the spell took. Waste of a good paper, if you ask me."

Arthur remembered the vacancy for the bedsit he'd seen posted up in the newsagent's window. There had been no mention of having to live with acts of witchcraft, perhaps involving the Birmingham Mail. That, on top of news of the murderer, only increased his disquiet with the day. He could put himself back on the path of normality with something to eat and a sleep. He had to remove himself from Ethel's company as quickly as possible. In that moment, the whole of his sanity seemed to rest on accomplishing the seemingly simple task. "I must get to bed," he said.

"That's right, my dear, you work nights," Ethel said.

"So if you don't mind."

"Mind? Of course not! Why would I mind?"

"Good night to you then."

Ethel smiled at him, immovable. "A good morning to you, my dear."

Arthur clenched the newspaper in his hand. Would Ethel retrieve the newspaper from the dustbin? Was she the type to rummage through another person's rubbish? He'd take the chance that Ethel would respect the privacy of his throwaways. The dustbin lid had his name on it, after all. His rubbish was his rubbish and nobody else's rubbish. He dropped the newspaper into the dustbin, and then he picked up the fallen dustbin lid from the ground and once and for all covered up the newspaper, out of sight to be hopefully out of mind, too. However, as he walked away from Ethel and towards the house, he surely heard that same dustbin lid being raised and then again put back into place. He didn't have it in him to find out if that was the case.

***

Arthur made it around to the back of the house, thinking of Ethel reading the story about the murderer, before she moved onto reading the classifieds, while he soon tried to sleep. The weight of the thoughts layered upon the weariness of his body after packing pallet after pallet with bottled and jarred sauces and pickles and mustards and relishes throughout the night. As jobs went, it wasn't the worst he could think of, but it certainly wasn't the best either. How long he could last out was a cause for worry, though. He'd seen his supervisor watching him from afar, checking in on how fast he was finding items throughout the warehouse and then placing them on each pallet to be shrink-wrapped and driven to shops across town. He'd only broken one bottle of brown sauce that night's shift, which was a marked improvement on previous shifts. His supervisor had written something down in a black notepad on witnessing the breakage. He imagined it wasn't a favourable comment on his work. Had it been worse than the other notes? It was cold-going-on-freezing in the warehouse and he couldn't right now afford to buy the clothes to keep the coldness out of him. Was it any wonder that his shivering would lead to him dropping the bottle of brown sauce? How many notes would it take before there were too many breakages, and they let him go? Then there was the business about his supervisor telling him he wasn't where he was supposed to be when he was there all along. He didn't understand that at all. Did his supervisor need a new pair of glasses? The worry of it all! He needed the job to keep his bedsit. Though he was sure his supervisor didn't care about that, only about how many bottles of brown sauce he broke each night. He had to cling to a positive attitude. He had to push back his worries of murder and unemployment and homelessness to somewhere inside of him where they couldn't wrestle with his mind. Life really was on the up and up if he considered what he'd accomplished since moving down from Manchester. In quick fashion, he now had a new job and a new place to live. They were accomplishments he should be proud of and surely the start of better things to come. If only he would let it be. He couldn't allow himself to be his own worst enemy once more.

On his way to the tenants' back door entrance, Arthur navigated a winding, moss-covered stone slab path encroached upon by shrubbery in desperate need of a pruning and over which hung the grabbing branches of gnarly apple trees. He wouldn't have minded the way into the house so much, as he did like a bit of nature, if it weren't for the many lifesize Grecian statues that populated the back garden, lurking behind the apple trees and popping up out of assorted vegetation when he least expected. He supposed the statues had once been pristine porcelain white, but those glory days were long gone. Now the statues were in what he'd have to say was a rampant state of devilishness, with faces cracked and disturbingly angular and bodies draped in raggedy moss, the colour of which was one for turning away from rather than for pleasant admiration. If ever a murderer, a brutal murderer, wanted to blend into the scenery, waiting for an unsuspecting person to jump upon and take down, this was certainly the garden for encouraging that kind of black-hearted intent. This, though, wasn't a rational thought and Arthur muttered a few reprimanding words to himself for entertaining the idea that the murderer would pay him a visit over everybody else living in the United Kingdom's second largest city. With all those people, surely a huge number lined up ahead of him for being brutally murdered? That, and he'd only just moved back to Birmingham. The murderer was probably under the impression that he still lived in Manchester. That was more like it. That was the way to think. He was perfectly safe and there was nothing to worry about. With this reasoning shoring up his peace of mind, he turned a corner of the garden path to see a crumbling face appear from out of a bush, with eyes that were mad with beetles. He yelped and dashed for the sanctuary of the house's inside.

***

Within the house, Arthur breathed a sigh of relief, taking in through his nostrils the smell of the building, which was one of musty oldness usually mixed with whatever had been prepared for meals by the other tenants and the two sisters, Ethel and Mildred. That morning there was a pervading and pungent aroma of fish, perhaps kippers, that had fought and won over the smells of all other breakfasts handsomely. Arthur's nose contorted with repugnance. Even if he weren't vegetarian, he wouldn't have touched fish, especially kippers, with a ten-foot barge pole. If there was one thing he could say about his regular and favourite meal of baked beans on toast, it didn't leave the house crying out for fumigation. "There should be some rule against fish," he said to himself, as he climbed the first of two flights of stairs that would lead him upwards and ever upwards to his attic bedsit. As he went, he tried to keep his eyes firmly set on the purple threadbare carpet in front of him rather than on the many framed portraits hung up on the wall to his right. When Ethel had first taken him up the stairs to show him the bedsit he'd come inquiring about, she'd stopped now and then to tell him about the portraits, all of which she'd painted, and all of which were of former tenants of the house. He'd never seen such a gallery of worrying faces. He preferred to think that it was only Ethel's artistic eye that had given her subjects such faces rather than they actually looked like that in real life. Each face appeared ready for prolonged care at a health resort. Had the oil paints really slipped and slopped over the canvases to imbue the various faces with a terrible movement? "I've painted all our dearly departed, except one," Ethel had said to him. "Now, even when they're gone, they're here, except the one we wanted to go." Then, two steps above him, Ethel had looked down onto his own face for a long and quiet minute, seemingly, to him anyway, trying to crawl back behind his eyes to have a good poke around, and had said, "When your time's up, I'll paint you, my dear." Ethel and her sister, Mildred, must've been in the business of renting out bedsits for decades as the wall displayed going on fifty-or-so tenant portraits, though he'd never dare to count the exact number, the accumulation of which gave the wall the appearance of a football stand packed with supporters. Yes, he'd keep his eyes on the stair carpet, as he'd done so from the day he'd moved into the house. There were his shoes. His only pair of shoes. Goodness, he needed a new pair of shoes. They were as worn out as the stair carpet beneath them. An embarrassment, they were. Even people on the street asking for money would let him pass by without a word upon seeing his shoes. They knew there wouldn't be a penny from him. He'd buy a new pair with his first wage packet. Maybe two pairs: a pair for work and a pair for going down to the shops. Nothing fancy. He wouldn't be able to afford fancy. Would they dock his wages to pay for the broken bottles of brown sauce? Maybe he'd only be able to buy one pair of shoes? It would have to be the work pair. A vigorous pair. A pair that would protect his feet, as well as they could for the money he'd be able to spend on them, from speeding forklift trucks, falling pallets, and smashing brown sauce bottles. What would become of him if he lost a foot working? He'd get the boot from his job the same day. That's what would happen. His life would then cascade into misery from that point onwards. If only he'd been able to get an office job. How he'd applied! How he'd heard nothing back! With an office job, he'd have been able to park his feet safely beneath a desk.

At the top of the stairs, Arthur thought he heard the painted faces of the people who once lived in the house turn on mass to watch him go. He wasn't sure of the sound of paint moving, or if paint moving even had a sound, but what he heard could've only been that sound. Yes? No. Absolutely not. He wouldn't think any more about it. What was he doing to himself? He was exhausted and famished, that was all. Two conditions that were certainly enough to prick out of his imagination unhealthy auditory phenomena for him to ponder. Either way, he was glad to have the stairs and the portraits behind him, for the time being at least. Ahead of him now was a short orange carpeted hallway that rose and sunk in places like a raised relief map of a mountainous land. Thankfully for him, the walls here were free from the painted faces of previous tenants. Only a large, oval mirror hung on the wall to the left of him. A mirror that had a sparkly, crystalline appearance so that when he would pass, he saw what he could only describe as the apparition of himself. The first time he'd seen his ghostly reflection, he'd given himself such a start that he was glad nobody was around to see and comment upon his fright. A little past the mirror was a cream door ornately painted with a gold number one, the brush strokes speaking of Ethel's handiwork, of that he was sure. Whenever he passed another tenant's bedsit door, he preferred to hurry so as to save himself from brief greetings or, worse, extended conversation with the occupant. So he hurried, along the hallway and out onto and across a sizeable landing, upon which lived two other tenants, and where the shared bathroom was situated, and up and up a twisting flight of stairs, high into the house, where the retreat of his bedsit awaited, a gold number five painted on the cream door.

***

Before Arthur could lay a hand on his door keys, his next-door neighbour, who lived across a small octagonal landing from him, appeared as if by a magician's trick, holding her handbag as though it were a hatchet. He'd only spoken to the woman a handful times, his conversations with her made up of awkward hellos and quick goodbyes. Her name was Debbie, or Betty. No, it was Debbie; he was sure of it. He backed away from her. Why was she approaching him in a manner that strongly suggested she'd something to say and she was going to say it, or there'd be the devil to pay?

Arthur backed himself against his bedsit door, worried about being struck by his neighbour's handbag, which had sharp-looking metal corners that could conceivably cause worrying damage in the right hands. Perhaps Debbie was the brutal murderer terrorising the poor people of Birmingham? Her face was murderous enough to fit the bill. No, it couldn't be. Could it be? He thought about breathing. In particular, a breathing exercise a therapist had once taught him that would calm himself down in stressful situations. Now, how did it go again? Yes, that was it. Breathe in through your nose. Let your belly fill with air. Breathe out through your nose. Once done, repeat another three times.

Debbie jabbed her handbag in Arthur's direction. "Knock! Knock! All night long! A bird, too!"

In response, Arthur continued with his breathing exercise. He could see that Debbie was expecting him to say something and that her patience for hearing from him was on a hot burner, about to bubble over.

"You work nights, yeah?" Debbie asked.

Arthur nodded in the affirmative while taking his final deep breath in through his nose. The therapist he'd seen must've been a charlatan, as the breathing exercise wasn't relieving his stress. Instead, it was only bringing on a bout of dizziness.

"Well, tell your caller that," Debbie said.

"Caller?" The word fairly lept from out of Arthur's mouth. Who'd be calling on him? He didn't know anybody well enough to have a caller. What had they wanted? What had he done?"Knock! Knock! A caller!" Debbie said.

Arthur was afraid to ask, but he wouldn't have been able to catch a wink of sleep wondering who the person was that had been knocking at his door while he'd been at work. "Who was it?"

Debbie huffed. "I don't know. Do I look like your help?"

Arthur wasn't sure, but had a look of fear broken through the ramparts of his neighbour's combative face with her reply? He'd never know for certain, as then she was storming off down the stairs with her last words on the matter loud enough for the entire house to hear, let alone him: "If it happens again, expect the worst!"

***

With a click, clack, and a clunk, Arthur locked himself away inside of his bedsit. It was a new home that was nothing much to look at, but it did him good to look at it all the same. When he'd first seen the room, fashioned within the roof of the house, all he could think of was that the builders must've done a spot of undertaker's work on the side as the shape of the room, without question, was that of a coffin. At the narrower end of the room, where a person's feet would rest, was the door, to the left of which was a corner wash sink, and to the right of which was a cooker, from which the walls tapered like the lines of a human body to the far end of the room, the head end, where a single bed was situated, to the right of which was a writing desk. Between the door and the bed, where a person's legs, arms, and torso would be, either pushed to the sides, or pushed out a little way, were a wardrobe, a two-person sofa, an electric fire, and a small breakfast table with a solitary chair, the table decorated with a potted white-flowered primrose he'd brought with him from Manchester. All of that and a covered bird cage atop a tall stand.

"Sunny, I'm home," Arthur said, walking over to the wardrobe where he placed his backpack and hung up his coat. "Are you sleeping in? I'm not surprised. Awake all night, I hear!"

Sunny was company that felt right to Arthur at this point in his life, a yellow canary that he'd found abandoned on the high street not long after he'd moved into the bedsit. The poor bird had been flapping about in its cage in obvious distress, compounded by the noise of passing people and cars, no one noticing, no one caring to help. He'd noticed. He'd cared. Of course, he hadn't known the bird's name, or even if the bird had a name, so he'd named it Sunny not only for its bright yellow colour but also because the sun had been shining down on him and the bird that day, making it the sunny side of the street, like the song goes. On bringing Sunny home, Ethel had told him that while they didn't allow their tenants to keep pets, she'd make an exception for Sunny given the circumstances of the bird's existence so far, adding the proviso that Sunny shouldn't bother the other tenants. Arthur thought of Debbie. It wasn't Sunny's fault there'd been all that knocking at his door. He would've fallen into conniptions if he'd been at home, too. However, that was then, and now there wasn't a peep from Sunny. "See, you're a good little bird," Arthur said, removing the birdcage covering. "Aren't you?"

Arthur dropped the birdcage cover to the floor and put a hand to his mouth where a scream sounded out as best it could through the gaps in his fingers. There, lying at the bottom of the cage, was a silent and still Sunny, a patch of red staining yellow feathers where a heart once beat. Arthur's whole body stuttered and then wobbled and then he fell to the floor. Next, he heard a knock, knock at his door. Then, after a moment, another knock, knock. The caller! Back again! Was it? That's what Debbie had said to him: "Knock! Knock! All night long!" A caller for terrorising Sunny. A caller for terrorising him! He placed a hand over his heart that was now beating with a ferocious rhythm. It was the murderer! The murderer who'd killed all those people. The murderer who'd killed Sunny. Knock! Knock! A murderer who now wanted to murder him. Knock! Knock! From his position on the floor, something slipped beneath his door, slowly at first and then hurriedly in a pushed way. It was a newspaper. The Birmingham Mail. The knock-knocking at his door stopped. In its place, he heard Ethel's voice from behind his door: "Here's your paper back in case you forgot to read the classifieds." He then heard Ethel walk away. Arthur couldn't take his eyes off the newspaper. From his position down on the floor, he could read the Birmingham Mail's front-page subheading: **WHERE ARE THE VICTIMS' HEADS?** Arthur gulped and impulsively checked to see if his own head hadn't gotten away from him. Of course it hadn't. He ought to be carted off for such daft thinking. Still, given everything the morning had thrown at him so far, he could pardon himself for ensuring everything on the outside of him was all where it should be. As for the inside of him, that being the inside of his head in particular, well, that was a different diagnosis altogether. He looked away from the newspaper. Above him, he saw Sunny's birdcage.

***

At the breakfast table, Arthur guiltily ate his baked beans on toast and drank a mug of tea. He'd wondered if he'd have an appetite after caring for Sunny, but afterwards his stomach had moaned out for a meal. It had been over eight hours since he'd eaten his cheese sandwich. He'd hoped Sunny wouldn't mind him eating. That, of course, meant baked beans on toast. Tins of baked beans, a block of cheddar cheese, and sliced white bread for toasting and sandwiches were all that he'd to eat in the bedsit. He wasn't an imaginative food shopper. Besides, imaginative food shopping meant money in his pocket that he didn't have. Luckily for him, however, he enjoyed baked beans on toast. If he were to rank his favourite meals, baked beans on toast would be up there in his top three, sometimes in first place, other times in second place, occasionally in third place, but forever and always in his top three. He especially liked the way the beans dressed in their tomato sauce clothing would go about the business of making the buttered toast soggy and limp, so that the toast didn't resemble toast anymore, or even bread, a metamorphosis, which was, to him, and probably him alone, from the first to the last mouthful delicious.

"Beans on toast, Sunny," Arthur said, looking at the potted prim-rose there on the table in front of him where six-inches under the soil now rested Sunny, "there's nothing else quite like it for making you feel better than you were doing a moment ago. Not today, though."

Arthur reached out to touch one of the primrose's long velvety leaves. "It's a Streptocarpus, a Cape primrose, if you'd like to know. I'm sure you would," Arthur said. "It's been with me through some hard times. Like you were with me. For a short time, at least. Now you're both together. The two of you, friends."

Arthur ate the last of his beans on toast and drank the last of his tea. He stood up from the breakfast table. He supposed he should do the washing up. The sink seemed a country mile away. His bed was but a step or two.

Afternoon

Poor, poor Arthur was being sentenced for a crime unknown, or so was the predicament within his dream. He sat in the dock at the back of the courtroom, with a gold number five hanging around his neck, and watched helplessly as a motley cast of characters discussed his fate. A custody officer sat next to Arthur, pressing him back down into his seat whenever he tried to stand up and wave his hands in protest of the Crown Court's proceedings. Arthur knew it was a Crown Court, as there was a royal coat of arms mounted on the wall above the judge's bench. If that hadn't been a giveaway, he would've had no doubt where he was as the custody officer would say to him: "This is a Crown Court, so mind your Ps and Qs!" every time he made a nuisance of himself in the opinion of the custody officer, who was, without question, a giant baked bean complete with face, arms, and legs. The custody officer also restricted his attempts to appeal his case, not that he knew what he was appealing against, which made it difficult for him to know if the words he blurted out would benefit him, or only make matters worse. The custody officer silenced his basic human right to be heard not through the usual means, such as a punch to the nose, but with a tin of baked beans and a stainless steel spoon. Each time he opened his mouth to say something, such as "You've got the wrong man!" or "You only have to look at me to know I shouldn't be here!" the custody officer would spoon-feed him cold baked beans from the tin, so that all anybody could hear, he was sure of it, were the garbled ravings of a lunatic. The looks he received from the adjacent gallery observing the proceedings, which comprised Ethel's paintings of previous tenants, only proved that to be the case. After each spoonful of baked beans, the custody officer would ask him: "Now there, doesn't that make you feel better?"

Arthur, sick to the brim with baked beans, watched the prosecuting and defending barristers, wearing black gowns and white wigs, approach the judge's bench. He'd yet to see their faces, but something about the way they moved put him in mind of garden statues instilled with enough life for movement, but not enough life for that movement to be considered human. He wondered which of them was his barrister? Was it the one with ivy growing from beneath their gown? Or the one that evidently only possessed one arm? Did it really matter? "It doesn't matter," the custody officer said to him. "Nobody cares." The custody officer had an uncanny knack of knowing what he was thinking. He tried to comment on that, but baked beans spilled out of his mouth instead of words. Although he couldn't see the barristers' faces, he could see the judge's face. If he could call it a face, as the judge's face was but an all-seeing eye that opened like a mouth for speaking. While the judge spoke with the two barristers, the stenographer, who sat in front of the judge's bench, frantically typed all that was being said for posterity. He saw the stenographer was Ethel, and as her fingers clicked and clacked over the keys of the stenograph, a newspaper emerged from the machinery. The clerk of the court, who was his work supervisor, then handed over page after page of the newspaper to those sitting in the jury box, which comprised only four people, all of whom had gold door numbers hanging around their necks, one through four, one of the jurors being his next-door neighbour, Debbie. He didn't recognise the other three jurors, though he supposed they too were tenants of the house in which he lived, as one of them was eating a plate of kippers while reading the news of the court. The jurors read the pages of the newspaper with animated faces of shock and horror. Arthur supposed that meant he was in for bad news. What on earth had he done? He made it a point in his life to keep on the straight and narrow. It was then that the judge banged his gavel once and then twice, and the courtroom fell silent. With that, the custody officer said to Arthur: "Look lively, the verdict's in." Arthur did as he was told and stood, seeing the judge's vast eye turn from the colour of a clear blue sky to a sky overtaken by rolling, blackened clouds. The judge spoke with a deafening loudness that shook the chandeliers hanging from the courtroom ceiling, his pronouncement being: "We have our murderer! Into the flower pot with him!" Then, into the courtroom, beetles wearing black mourning suits and top hats wheeled a huge yellow flowering primrose growing from a huge terracotta pot. Arthur's response, with his words mangled by baked beans, was: "I really have to go to the loo." Thankfully, it was a bodily function urgent enough to wake him and remove himself from the courtroom and place him back into his bed, damp with cold sweat.

***

Arthur put on his dressing gown and slippers and left his bedsit for the loo. The dream, no, a nightmare, followed him down the stairs, attached, nagging away at his consciousness. Perhaps he'd eaten a bad tin of baked beans for breakfast? It was the cheaper kind he'd been buying. Who knew what pride the company took in producing one of the country's favourite convenience foods? Did they have a quality control department? Or didn't they care one jot that bad cans of baked beans were being shipped throughout the United Kingdom to terrorise their customers' sleep? Accusing them of murder! He'd a good mind to call the manufacturer's customer service department and lodge a complaint. He supposed he'd need proof that the baked beans caused his nightmare. How would he come about that? There wasn't a baked bean left to test. He'd eaten them all. So many in his nightmare, too! It was enough to put someone, someone other than him, off baked beans for life.

At the bottom of the stairs, Arthur hurried across the house's second floor landing so as not to inadvertently meet the two tenants who lived on the floor, if they were at home. The carpeted floor and his slippers softened his presence. On reaching the bathroom door, with no tenant disturbed, he went to turn the bathroom doorknob and found the door locked. "Just a moment. Nearly done," came a voice from inside of the bathroom. Arthur knew that one day this would happen. Fortunately, he'd had access to the bathroom whenever he'd liked since moving into the house. There had been the time when he was having a bath when someone else from the house wanted in, like he now wanted in, but they had gone away and left him in peace. Should he go away and come back? He could hide some way up the stairs and listen for the person to leave the bathroom. Then he could return. In this way, he wouldn't have to make conversation. It seemed a reasonable plan, the best of plans. He'd have to hurry, though. The person had said they were nearly done, which meant they'd soon be opening the bathroom door. He'd no idea what he would say in the situation. His silence would likely force the person into scrutinising his presence, and they'd notice the large hole in his dressing gown showing his pyjamas. He didn't want anybody seeing his pyjamas.

He didn't want anybody seeing him. If only he were back in his bed, asleep, free of nightmares, and not wanting the loo. Then, in all of his prevarication, the bathroom door opened, and there, suddenly standing before him, was a woman, about his age, wearing a dressing gown. She smelled of kippers.

Arthur found his slippered feet rooted to the carpet. He considered that the woman hadn't been 'nearly done' at all. She'd been quicker than what he'd consider 'nearly done'. She'd been more 'on her way out', he'd have to say. If she'd said that she'd been on her way out, he could've been up the stairs by now. There was one other thing for Arthur to think upon, too, and that was that the woman looked a lot like one juror from his nightmare. Juror number three. The woman cinched her dressing gown at the neck and looked for a way past Arthur. Noticing the woman's need to go about her morning business without chatter, Arthur obligingly moved to the left to let the woman pass. At that moment, the woman took it upon herself to move to the left, too. Arthur gave the woman an apologetic smile. In return, the woman frowned at Arthur. Again Arthur smiled at the woman, and again the woman frowned at Arthur. Ill at ease, Arthur moved to the right to once again let the woman pass. The woman moved to the right as well. Behind the woman, Arthur could see the loo at the far end of the bathroom. If only he could stand in front of it instead of standing in front of the woman! How did he ever get himself into such situations? It wasn't as if he tried to give himself a continually hard time in living. He had to wonder if there was something amiss within him, like a loose bolt, a stuck lever, or perhaps a blocked pipe. Had he come off the assembly line built this way? Not properly put together? As long back as he could remember, this had been the way he'd operated: out of time and out of step with the rest of humanity. What a life he had to keep up and lead! All he wanted was to go to the loo. Did everything, even the simplest of things, have to be fraught with angst and a hint of danger? The woman looked at him as though he were some type of criminal. No. She looked at him as though he were a murderer, no less. He could see fear colouring her eyes. It seemed as if the yellow plastic rollers in her black hair positively twitched with panic. Had she been reading the newspaper, too? He had to make it clear to the woman that her head was safe on her shoulders. He took a step to the left to give the woman some breathing room, and him some room for words to come out of him freely. The woman stepped to the left, too.

Arthur panicked. "I'm not the murderer, you know," he said, and with that, the woman pushed past him as though her life depended on it.

"Tell that to the court," the woman said, quick to her bedsit door. "Standing there flashing your pyjamas at me."

"It's a hole in my dressing gown," Arthur said, lifting his dressing gown up to show a large ripped piece of brown chequered cloth in dire need of a darning, but the woman had already shut herself away in her bedsit.

Arthur stood outside of the bathroom in two minds about what to do next. He supposed he could knock on the woman's door to explain himself. Frankly, though, that was the last thing he wanted to do and would likely bring him a visit from the police, he was sure. Instead, he went to the loo. While going, it worried him deeply that the woman may've dreamt of his nightmare trial, too. Could things like that happen? Surely not. She'd looked the spitting image of juror number three. She'd told him: "Tell that to the court." Thinking about this made going to the loo difficult.

***

Arthur's mobile phone rang when he was about to get back into bed, giving him a significant start. After his heart had settled back into its usual place in his chest, he made a mental note to change the ringtone to something a little less like the music used in horror movies for when the cat leaps out of a cupboard, scaring the teens exploring the old, spooky house. Who'd call him? Who even had his phone number? The sisters had his phone number. He'd written it down on the six-month lease for the bedsit. Why would one of them be calling him? They could come and speak to him face-to-face whenever they cared. Who else? Arthur sank down to sit on the edge of his bed. Work had his phone number, too. If it wasn't the sisters calling him, it must be work. No one else had his number. Across the room, on the table next to Sunny's final resting place beneath the potted primrose, the phone continued to ring. Cat after cat jumping out of cupboards through-out the haunted house. It was a pink phone. A cheap pay-as-you-go model. It was all he could afford. He wished it wasn't pink. He hadn't the money for the next model up, the one in black. The man at the newsagent who'd taken his money for the phone had said to him: "I remember the day I bought my daughter her first phone. They grow up so quickly, don't they?" He didn't have the courage to reply that the phone was for his own use. The phone stopped ringing. Then, after a moment or two, the phone buzzed. Work had left a message for him.

Arthur knew he wouldn't be able to get back to sleep, knowing that work had left him a message. He'd lay there in bed wondering what the message could be, and it wouldn't be a favourable message such as he was going to be given more hours, or that management had been so impressed with his performance they were going to reward him with a bump in pay. More likely, the message would be that his pay was going to be docked for all the bottles of brown sauce he'd broken, or that management was so unimpressed with his performance that he shouldn't bother coming in that evening or any evening afterwards. How could he sleep knowing there was a message like that waiting for him on his phone? If he could sleep, he knew his subconscious would only fashion another nightmare for him to endure, most likely worse than the courtroom nightmare. He stood up from the bed and walked over to the phone with a deepening sense of dread. He remembered the time his secondary school maths teacher had asked him to come to the front of class to solve a chalked algebra problem on the blackboard. That day, he'd walked to the blackboard knowing only bad news waited for him once he reached the blackboard. He hadn't a clue on how to solve the algebra problem. To him, letters had no right being mixed with numbers, and whoever had come up with the bright idea of doing so was patently a sadist with a hatred for secondary school children, particularly himself. Once he'd reached the blackboard, feeling the teacher's eyes boring holes into his body and hearing sniggers from his classmates, he made a hard left for the classroom door, which he opened to carry on walking out of the classroom, out of the school, and all the way home. When his mom had asked him why he wasn't at school, he didn't have an answer. The last thing he remembered was seeing the algebra problem on the blackboard, coming alive, twisting and turning, a labyrinth of complications. He'd no recollection of anything that had happened thereafter. This, he explained to his mom. "Don't say you're back at it again," his mom had replied. He hadn't known what she'd meant.

So it was that Arthur, on his way to his phone, fell into that same dream-like state, not part of the world, but not apart from it, either. On reaching the table, close enough to pick up his phone, he drifted away and away towards his bedsit door. As he was unlocking and opening the door, there came a knock, knock upon it. The two knocks were enough to bring Arthur out from beneath whatever hypnotic state he'd fallen. Two police officers confronted him.

***

Arthur sat on his sofa, while one of the police officers sat in the solitary breakfast table chair, facing him, jotting down words in a black notepad. The other police officer, for want of anywhere else to sit other than Arthur's bed, stood in front of the closed bedsit door reading Arthur's Birmingham Mail.

The sitting police officer looked up from his notepad and fixed Arthur to the sofa with a stare. "Lived in Birmingham long?"

"I've just moved here," Arthur said.

"Where from?"

"Manchester." The police officer huffed and wrote in his notepad. "You arrived when?"

"Three weeks ago."

"I see."

Arthur didn't like the way the police officer had said, I see. Worry poured into his body, gelling about his internal bodily functions. Suddenly, his breathing didn't feel proper.

"You arrived in Birmingham just before the murders started. I see," the sitting police officer said.

"I work nights," Arthur said, knowing from reading the newspaper that each of the murders had occurred during his work hours.

"I'm not asking you for an alibi, Mr. Underwood," the sitting police officer said. "Where do you work, exactly?"

Arthur gave up the information freely and watched as it was all written in the black notepad. His work supervisor used the same kind of black notepad to write things about him, too.

"You know about the murders?" the sitting police officer asked.

"He's keeping up with the grizzly details," the standing police officer said, not looking up from the insides of the Birmingham Mail.

"You can't think…" Arthur said, his words trailing into silence.

"We're only asking questions, Mr. Underwood. It's part of the job, you know. We ask questions and you provide the answers. I'm sure you've seen how it happens on the TV. Ever seen that?"

"I don't have a TV."

The sitting police officer looked about Arthur's bedsit. "No radio or books that I can see, either. How do you keep yourself entertained, Mr. Underwood?"

"Frightening poor defenceless women," the standing police officer said, turning a page of the Birmingham Mail.

"Ms. Thomas, your downstairs neighbour, recounts a harrowing tale of your meeting earlier," the sitting police officer said.

"It's a big misunderstanding," Arthur said. "All I wanted was to go to the bathroom."

"Ms. Thomas said you exposed yourself to her," the sitting police officer said.

"It was only my pyjamas. There's a hole in my dressing gown. She saw through."

"Does that make it any better, Mr. Underwood? Some women aren't used to seeing men's pyjamas. Ms. Thomas is one of those women. You might have shown her what's under your pyjamas for all the difference it makes. Then, of course, there's the matter of you telling Ms. Thomas that you were the murderer. The murderer we're all looking for, possibly?"

"I said that I wasn't the murderer!"

"Now, why would you even think of saying such a thing?"

"It just came out."

"Like your pyjamas, perhaps?"

"Yes. I mean, no. She misheard me."

"Ms. Thomas seemed fine of hearing to me."

"I'm not the murderer! I only wanted to go to the bathroom!"

Arthur watched the sitting police officer write a flurry of words into his black notepad, vigorously underling something three times.

"That will be all for now, Mr. Underwood."

"There'll be more?" Arthur asked.

With an answer to Arthur's question unforthcoming, the two police officers departed, though not before the standing police officer had returned the Birmingham Mail into Arthur's safekeeping.

Arthur looked at the newspaper, now rearranged to show the classified ads section. One particular advertisement above all the others caught his attention: **DESIRABLE AND AFFORDABLE SUTTON COLDFIELD ATTIC BEDSIT FOR RENT. AVAILABLE SOON. DON'T MISS OUT. CALL ETHEL AT—**

Arthur stopped reading. Word for word, it was the same classified ad he'd seen three weeks ago in calling up about his own bedsit. Surely it couldn't be the same bedsit? The same Ethel? Why would his bedsit be available soon? He hurried over to his desk and, from a drawer, pulled out his rental agreement. Turning over pages, he found Ethel's phone number. It was the same phone number listed in the classified ad. Ethel had told him you never know what you might turn up in the classifieds that's worth knowing. Hadn't she?

***

Arthur ate a piece of a Victoria sponge cake and then drank some of his tea. It was as though Ethel and Mildred had been expecting him to call. From the moment he'd rung the doorbell at the front of the house, his welcome had been the kind usually reserved for old and dear friends, or someone perhaps delivering a large amount of money. The two sisters had led him through the expansive ground floor of the house and seated him in a room, in which no space, neither the floor nor the walls, was left untouched by furniture, pictures, photo frames, books, newspapers, lighting fixtures, and various and multitude objets d'art. One time, looking up from his Victoria sponge, Arthur had thought that Ethel and Mildred had got up and left him in the room all by himself, such was the distracting clutter of the room, but then his eyes had refocused and there Ethel and Mildred were after all, the two of them perched side-by-side on the edge of a sofa, like two wizened and weather-beaten gargoyles. What the sisters had told him so far hadn't made an awful lot of sense; it had all been far-fetched, to be believed by a person for whom insanity was a regular bedfellow. To add to that, Ethel was now at her easel painting him as he sat in an overstuffed armchair, his plated slice of Victoria sponge cake and cup of tea resting on his lap. Of course, he'd attempted to resist this turn of events, but Ethel's persuasion had been the equivalent of turning the armchair in which he sat into a warm and relaxing bubble bath. While that was happening, Mildred remained on the sofa, explaining to him once again the days past, the day present, and, for good measure, the days future. As he listened, Arthur felt Mildred's words making more and more sense. Insanity, he felt, was indeed creeping up on him from all directions with the Victoria sponge and cup of tea weighed heavily upon his lap, making an escape from his bathtub impossible.

"I see all of our tenants coming and going, as I saw you coming and going," Mildred said. "I tried to help, but the spell didn't take.

Sometimes it's that way. The spell turns out, or it doesn't. Like a Yorkshire pudding."

Arthur fumbled with his cup and saucer, spilling tea onto his trousers.

"Try to keep still. I've nearly captured you," Ethel said, her paintbrush slipping and sliding over canvas.

"Sorry," Arthur said.

"Don't be sorry," Mildred said. "We're all born to live and die."

"I don't want to die," Arthur said.

Mildred looked upwards to the ceiling, and then seemingly through wood and plaster farther and farther upwards into the house. "The murderer is with us. Your murderer, Arthur."

Arthur looked upwards, too. "Why me?"

Mildred sighed. "Why any of us?"

"There, finished," Ethel said, putting her paintbrush down. "Who wants to see?"

"I do," Mildred said, wrestling herself from the sofa with the aid of a walking stick. Crunched over, she hobbled over to see Arthur's portrait. "Oh, I like the eyes. If the murderer was calling on me, those would be my eyes."

Ethel and Mildred stared at Arthur.

"You, too," Ethel said. "Up you get. Come and see."

"I'd rather not," Arthur said.

"Not even out of curiosity?" Ethel asked.

"Not even for fun?" Mildred asked.

"Please, no," Arthur said.

Mildred put her arm around Ethel, as much to steady herself as to congratulate her sister on a job well done. "It'll look lovely with the others."

Ethel smiled. "I think it's one of my best."

"Hello," Arthur said, waving at the sisters.

"You're still here," Ethel said.

"What am I supposed to do?" Arthur asked.

"You could leave," Ethel said. "Maybe that would help."

"I've nowhere else to go," Arthur said.

"Now you've lost your job. How do you expect to keep up your room?" Mildred asked.

Arthur thought about the phone call he'd received. "I tried my best."

"Perhaps something in an office this time," Mildred said. "There'd be no bottles of brown sauce to break."

"We do like you," Ethel said.

"We want you to stay on," Mildred said.

"Then please help me," Arthur said.

The sisters looked at each other and then at Arthur.

"There's the police," Ethel said.

"The police think I'm the murderer," Arthur said.

"It puts a spanner in the works," Mildred said.

"What a pickle," Ethel said.

Mildred jabbed her walking stick in Arthur's direction. "Here's a trick. Don't, on any account, answer your caller!"

"Careful, Mildred," Ethel said, catching hold of her sister, preventing her from toppling over. "You'll do yourself another mischief."

"Poor Sunny," Mildred said, safely wrapped up in Ethel's arms. "Wrong place at the wrong time. He wasn't to know."

***

Arthur had walked away from Ethel and Mildred and the house in a trance of sorts and had kept on walking and walking. Now, jolted from his hypnotic state by a group of kids hurling obscenities at him, he didn't know where he'd ended up walking, his surroundings—the houses, the trees, the lampposts—strangers with faces darkening as the sky darkened, asking him why he was where he was. He didn't have an answer. Now, confused and desperate to find some certainty of placement, he hurried through a street-on-street maze of terraced housing, lights being switched on downstairs and upstairs. The people inside the houses knew where they were. If only he could be one of them. Up ahead, a woman appeared from around a street corner. She hurried towards him, her high heels click-clicking over the pavement. He could ask her for directions to the nearest bus stop, for a bus to take him back to familiarity, but he'd let her pass on without saying a word. Any sentences he could string together would only jumble themselves up, likely bringing about screams from the woman, followed by multiple phone calls to the police from people inside of the houses. After his earlier run-in with the police, there'd be no coming back from that situation. They'd lock him away and throw away the key. He'd keep his head down, keep on walking straight ahead, taking care to give the woman enough room to go on about her business without fear of harassment. He wouldn't bother the woman, and the woman wouldn't bother him. His heart raced as the woman's high heels gave her away as being closer and closer. He wondered why he was suddenly having difficulty walking a straight line. Couldn't he do anything correctly? It was as though someone had switched his legs out for another's legs and the fit wasn't taking. If he were to walk into the woman, it would all be over. To what pitch of fear would that event drive him? Would he be a flurry of apologies? Would he run? Would he put his hands around the woman's neck to strangle the outrage from her? There was murder in everyone, after all. Wasn't there? The police had written him down for a murderer into a black notepad. But he wasn't the murderer they were looking for. He could be a different murderer, though. That would complicate matters for them down at the station. It would serve them right. For a moment, the click-clicking of the woman's high heels was a thunder in his ears. If only he could take charge of the leg that wanted to go left and the leg that wanted to go right, then perhaps he wouldn't be on the front page of tomorrow's Birmingham Mail. He didn't want to be a murderer. It sounded like a stressful occupation. He'd enough worry and anxiety in his life without foolishly pouring more into himself. Then the high-heel thunder rolled over and away until all he heard was the wind picking up and the pitter-patter of rain. The woman had gone wherever she was going. He couldn't help thinking: take me with you.

***

If ever there was a bus shelter, with a bus arriving soon enough to carry him back to familiarity, they'd hid it from Arthur. Sopping wet from a rain that had passed from light to heavy with alarming haste, Arthur took a shortcut through a children's playground for a bus shelter, any bus shelter, for a bus to take him this way, that way, whatever way, it didn't matter anymore. Inconveniently, there was no signpost for his new direction being a shortcut. Such was his desperation for a portal of speediness. He'd taken the promise of the children's playground being a shortcut with a mixture of faith and instinct only. Through the playground, he passed a crooked house, out of which he heard someone say to him: "Hey, mate. Get in here with me." He stopped on hearing the voice, male and gruff. There may've been no shortcut sign, but the voice was a sign large and loud enough to be a stop sign.

"My name's Brian," Brian said from inside of the crooked house. "What's yours?"

Arthur gave up his name freely, rather relieved to have come across another person; it had begun to feel that human existence, aside from him, had washed away in all of the rain.

"Come on then, Arthur, get yourself inside here with me," Brian said. "What's keeping you?"

Arthur could see Brian peering out at him from one of the crooked windows in the crooked house. Brian's face was mostly a beard. He didn't look the type of person he wanted to join inside of a crooked house.

"There's room enough for two," Brian said.

"I've got a bus to catch," Arthur said.

Brian laughed. "Good luck with that."

"What do you mean?" Arthur asked, disturbed by Brian's laugh.

"The buses won't stop. They don't see me. They won't see you by the looks of you," Brian said. "You'll want to get in here with me."

"I think I'm all right," Arthur said.

"You don't look all right."

Arthur looked past the crooked house, past the swing, past the slide, and to a gate that led out of the children's playground. "I'll be going then."

"Where?"

"Home."

"I had a home. Not this home. A bit like your home, maybe. Now this is my home."

"That's nice."

"You'd like it, too."

The rain continued to beat down on Arthur. "I don't think so."

"Dry in here," Brian said, banging a hand against the inside of the crooked house. "Well built by the sound of it, too."

Arthur looked longingly at the gate, a short rush and a push away from Brian. There'd be a bus shelter and not another crooked house beyond the gate. "Be seeing you," he said, hoping he'd never see Brian again.

"You won't," Brian said.

Once again, Brian's voice was enough of a stop sign to prevent Arthur from going on any farther, telling him he should really pay attention.

"We're a lot alike, me and you," Brian said.

"I don't have to talk to you," Arthur said.

"But you are."

"It's a mistake."

"Too many mistakes for the both of us. They all add up, you know. Gets to a point where you can't come back from all the mistakes made. They grab ahold of you. They put you where I am, where you are."

"I'd rather be where I am than where you are."

"You don't have to be in here with me for us to be both in the same place."

Arthur couldn't take it anymore. Why were people like Brian thrust into his life? All over, people all over were living normal lives without having to deal with the likes of Brian and Ethel and Mildred and the police and the murderer. He ran for the gate and as he ran he heard Brian shout: "There's more of us than you think, Arthur! And nobody cares! Nobody cares!"

Beyond the gate was indeed a bus shelter for Arthur. A bus coming. The number five. A number he knew. A bus he knew. He'd never felt this lucky in his life.

***

Arthur searched within his trouser pockets, but there was no money for a bus fare to be found. It wasn't as though he'd visited Ethel and Mildred thinking he'd need a couple of quid on him, just in case. Or, for that matter, had planned on leaving the house. Therefore, his coat, with his wallet stashed away inside, was still hanging up in the wardrobe. What was he to do? Perhaps the bus driver would be an understanding man? It wasn't like there was anyone else on the bus to complain about him getting on the bus for free when they'd had to pay for their ride.

"I've darts at eight," the bus driver said. "Can't idle all night here."

"I came out without my money," Arthur said.

"Came out without a coat on, too. You like the rain, do you?"

"Can I owe you?"

"Do I look like the Avon lady?"

"Never mind," Arthur said, turning away from the bus driver, stepping off the bus.

"You been crying?" the bus driver asked.

Arthur wiped his eyes. "It's the rain."

"You've got my Dot's eyes after she's turned on the waterworks."

"Good luck with the darts," Arthur said, walking away from the bus, along the pavement, puddles up over his shoes.

After a moment, the bus pulled up alongside Arthur. "You mean that?" the bus driver asked, looking out at Arthur, the door to the bus still open.

Arthur stopped. "Pardon?"

"The luck for my darts ," the bus driver said. "You mean it?"

"I hope you do well," Arthur said.

"I'm up against Big Barry. It's the quarters."

"Don't idle then," Arthur said, and then he carried on walking.

The bus driver matched the buse's pace with Arthur's pace. "You know your trouble," the bus driver said, "you give up too easily. Now get on, you daft bugger." The bus driver halted the bus.

Arthur looked up at the bus and the bus driver as though they were manna from heaven. "Really?"

"Don't be telling anyone back there I'm giving you a freebie," the bus driver said.

Arthur stepped onto the bus. "Thanks," he said.

"No need to be soppy about it," the bus driver said. "Now find yourself a seat. Only mind back there on the right. There's sick all over."

Arthur took a seat up front on the left. The bus driver pulled away.

"I nearly didn't stop for you," the bus driver said, "But don't tell the depot that."

"I'm glad you did," Arthur said.

"It was touch and go there for a while. First I didn't see you, and then I did see you. Then when I did see you, I nearly didn't stop for you what with a murderer on the loose. I'm not paid danger money. It's bad enough with the kids. The drunks. But a murderer! The life of a bus driver, I'll tell you. I'd be better off being one of those crash test dummies." The bus driver stopped at a traffic light and looked over his shoulder, back at Arthur. "You're not the murderer, are you?" He laughed. "Can't see it myself. That's why I stopped for you, I guess. I can spot trouble waiting a mile away. Gave you the benefit of the doubt, I did. It's just this murderer business has got me all shaken up. What happened to the heads? What does he do with the heads? And I say he, but the murderer could be a woman, right? My Dot nearly takes my head off every time I come home after one too many." He looked from Arthur back to the road ahead. The traffic light turned from red to green. The bus driver drove on. "What's your stop?"

Arthur told the bus driver where he wanted to get off.

"Big houses up there, and there's you with no money."

"It's a bedsit in a big house," Arthur said.

"Living the bachelor life, eh?" The bus driver chuckled. "Those were the days. Now there's Dot. She ain't a bad old sort. There's always pie and chips when I want them. You can't say every husband's got that going for them. Big Barry has to make his own pie and chips. That's probably why he's Big Barry. He's got the keys to the kitchen. Dot won't let me into our kitchen. Not after the great fry-up disaster of '86. Baked beans up on the ceiling, there were. Bacon fat over the cupboards. A black pudding in Dot's spider plant. She had me redecorating for a week."

Arthur wondered if the bus driver's ramblings were the reason for the bus having no one else aboard. Those people were likely all appearing when they knew the next bus was making an appearance. When the bus driver had asked if he was the murderer, the celebration within him of being on the bus had fizzled out so that all he knew was where the bus was taking him: back to his bedsit, Ethel and Mildred, and the murderer. He'd nearly told the bus driver a different stop for him all together. But what good would that have done him? As the bus driver had told him, he shouldn't give up so easily. There was more life in him yet. Maybe, like the bus driver, he'd marry his own Dot? How much life would he have to make it through to find a Dot that was like the bus driver's Dot? Someone to put up with all the madness that came along with being him, being Arthur? Right now, pie and chips sounded delicious. A cheese and onion pie, perhaps? He had more baked beans. How did beans end up on the ceiling during the great fry-up disaster of '86? He couldn't imagine.

"Your stop's here," the bus driver said.

Arthur stood up from his seat and walked to the front of the bus.

"If I beat Big Barry tonight," the bus driver said, "the semis are next Friday. Come up and see me throw. Do you know the Soused Swan in Erdington? You can't miss it. There's a big sign up outside showing a swan with a pint in one wing and an axe in the other wing chasing a bunch of troublemakers out the pub door. What did the swan do with their heads after it took the axe to them? That's what *I* want to know."

Arthur didn't want to know.

Evening

Ethel's portrait of Arthur hung on the staircase wall, along with the many portraits of other tenants. As usual, Arthur began climbing the flight of stairs purposefully ignoring the portraits, as painted face after painted face performed their utmost to attract his attention, but three-quarters of the way up the staircase the smell of fresh oil paints had poked enough curiosity inside of him so that he'd turned to be confronted with his likeness. Profoundly, he'd regretted his curiosity. It was a grotesque portrait. A portrait of a man gone mad. A portrait of a man encountering his demise. And he was the man. Those were his eyes, painted with fear spiralling. That was his mouth, painted a black hole scream.

Arthur looked away from his portrait to see two other painted faces looking back at him, one a woman's face, one a man's face. The painted faces moved, colours no longer dry and fixed in place, but colours wet and animated, slipping and slopping over canvas. The painted faces spoke to him.

"Nice to have you join us," the woman said.

"It's not," the man said.

"Don't say that."

"I can't help what I say."

"We've got to be welcoming."

"He's ignored us since he moved in," the man said, the black of his pupil bleeding into the blue of his iris. "Why should I be welcoming? Why any of us?"

This question struck a chord with other painted faces across the staircase wall, and they shouted the chorus: "Why any of us? Why any of us? Why any of us?"

"Order, order," the woman said.

A hush fell over the staircase.

"Besides, he won't join us until he's gone," the man said, "like the rest of us are gone. See, he's standing there now. I see him. We all see him."

"We see him," became the new chorus up and down the staircase wall. "We see him. We see him."

"He'll be gone. We all know that," the woman said. "We were all seen, and then we were gone."

The painted faces agreed. "Seen and gone. Seen and gone. Seen and gone."

It was all too much for Arthur. "Please," he said, "let me go."

"He speaks to us," the man said. "'Let me go', he says."

Painted faces turned to each other and then back to Arthur. "Where? Where? Where?"

"Quiet," the woman said, "let him say more."

"More, more, more," came the new cry.

Arthur looked down the staircase and then back up the staircase, past so many faces looking back at him, younger and older, older and younger, and he thought: how much worse could it be if he was to join them when he was gone as they were gone. His life had to end up somewhere, after all. The bus driver said he shouldn't give up so easily.

But would here be worse than anywhere else? He would've liked to watch the bus driver in the semis after he'd beaten Big Barry, though.

"More, more, more," the cry continued.

"My name is Arthur," Arthur said.

A chant rose. "Arthur, Arthur, Arthur."

"Welcome, Arthur," the woman said.

"Don't keep me up at night. They all do," the man said. "Nobody cares."

Arthur walked the last of the stairs, hearing as he went: "Nobody cares. Nobody cares. Nobody cares." He thought of Brian.

***

Arthur knew that he'd perhaps twenty seconds of light available for him to make it from the hallway at the top of the house's first flight of stairs to being safely stashed away inside of his bedsit. If he dilly-dallied, meandered, or moped at this time of the evening, he'd plunge into a pool of thick and lapping darkness. To save on electricity, Ethel and Mildred had installed light switch timers throughout the tenants' portion of the house. They'd been stingy on the time setting, too. No sooner was a light switch turned on, then it was popping off again. It was really a household economy best suited to Olympians. Arthur understood that despite his body being perfectly crafted for fleet-of-foot activities, he wasn't the athletic sort by any stretch of the imagination. He remembered the reaction of Mr. Richard, his middle school gym teacher, when he'd been put out for school cross-country trials based purely on his appearance alone and had laboured in a long way last. On finishing, Mr. Richard had looked at him with a mixture of disappointment and betrayal, as though he were on the verge of giving up teaching sports for teaching home economics. Mr. Richard had said to him: "There was certainly a balls-up down the factory the day you came off the assembly line." Afterwards, and back at home, he'd looked at himself in the bathroom mirror and poked about his torso, arms, and legs for wrong parts installed and correct parts not installed. It hadn't felt to him that he was made quite right.

Arthur placed a hand on the hallway light switch and tried to forget about Mr. Richard's diagnostic review of his body. There may've likely been a balls-up down the factory, but crossing the landing before the light went out wasn't the same as running three laps of a muddy, hilly park, while a gardener burned leaves nearby that turned breathing into the breathing usually associated with a person being given the last rites. His body was more than capable of the ordinary feat. Wasn't it? Though what ordinariness had frequented his day so far? What if he turned on the light and there was the murderer? What if he *didn't* turn on the light and the murderer was there? Mildred had looked upwards into the house as though to say the murderer was already with them, waiting for him. The painted faces were of the same opinion. He was here, but soon he'd be gone, they'd said. He was positive he could outrun a light switch turning off, but he couldn't outrun a murderer who'd pencilled his name into a black notepad. Though, perhaps the murderer was out of the house right now? They could be queuing for fish and chips, yes? Murderers had to eat like everyone else, after all. The murderer could even be at the Soused Swan, watching the bus driver play Big Barry at darts. He supposed a murderer would follow darts; what with the game involving three sharp objects that could take out a victim with three accurate throws. Maybe one throw with a bullseye. Then Arthur heard the tenants' door open at the foot of the stairs. "Who's that up there? I see your shadow," came a man's growly voice. "You better not be the murderer. Because if you're the murderer, I've a bag of Maris Pipers down here for your bollocks." Arthur switched on the landing light and the murderer wasn't to be seen ahead of him. He fled for his bedsit with lights quickly popping on and off and on and off and on and off behind.

***

As much as he wanted to sleep, Arthur couldn't sleep. He'd turned this way, that way, and the other way, searching for a light switch to turn himself off so that he could fall into nothingness, allowing his caller, the murderer, to take him in sweet and blissful slumber. All attempts in this direction had failed miserably, though. Now, for want of anything better to do, he paced back and forth within his bedsit, as much as the small bedsit allowed for pacing. A few steps, minding the electric fire, and he was at the door. A few steps, minding the electric fire, and he was beside his bed. Over and over, back and forth, he paced, a sentry guarding nothing of worth or interest. The police officer had been correct in his observations: he possessed nothing in the way of personal entertainment. He'd no distraction for a calming sedative to send him back to bed, to sleep. He'd no TV, no radio, no books, and his phone was only good for human contact, providing there'd be a human on the other end of the phone for contacting, which, when Arthur thought about it, was laughable. Not that he didn't want to watch what was on the TV, listen to a song on the radio, read a good book, or hear a familiar and friendly voice over the phone. It was only that his leaving Manchester for Birmingham had happened so fast and, with all that happened, it was hardly surprising he wasn't set up for a life of leisure. He supposed he could talk to Sunny. He wondered if his late friend was settling in well? The primrose looked a little more joyous for Sunny's presence. He hoped Sunny felt the same joy for his bedfellow, too. No, best leave Sunny to acclimate more. He didn't want to be a bother. He wondered who'd give him a sendoff after the murderer had called? There wouldn't be a queue forming for the job. And burials were expensive nowadays. Where would the money for his funeral come from? After losing his job, he didn't have enough money to keep a roof over his head, let alone a coffin lid. Urns were cheaper than coffins, weren't they? By how much? Coffin or urn, he supposed the bulk of funeral costs were down to labour and paperwork. A funeral couldn't take place without labour and paperwork. He couldn't afford labour and paperwork. Why couldn't the murderer visit a person who had enough money in their pocket for a regular and respectable funeral? A funeral of any kind? He remembered the courtroom beetles and the huge primrose growing from the huge terracotta pot. He shuddered. But if such a burial was good enough for Sunny, it would be good enough for him, yes?

Carrying thoughts of his own burial back and forth with him like so much heavy baggage, Arthur was once again reminded how much the bedsit resembled the shape of a coffin. How fitting that his last minutes that made up his last hours should tick on within a bedsit shaped like a coffin! Why was he thinking like that? Experience had told him to think like that! Mildred had told him he'd be safe if only he didn't answer the door when the murderer came knocking, which meant what?—that he shouldn't do something silly? The bus driver had told him he gave up too easily, which meant what?—that he should never give up hope? What did Mildred and the bus driver know of his life? Nothing, that's what! He was forever doing something silly. Silliness came as naturally to him as sensibility came naturally to the others. As for hope, that was for other people, not the likes of him. Hope didn't know he existed, unlike despair, which knew him intimately. He was no different from Brian. There Brian was within his crooked house, and here he was within a bedsit shaped like a coffin. "There's more of us than you think, Arthur! And nobody cares! Nobody cares!" Those were Brian's words. Brian spoke the truth. The painted faces spoke the truth, too. There was nothing that could be done. From beginning to end, cradle to grave, what was to transpire would transpire, written in a black notepad somewhere with concrete certainty and not a word for changing or for moving and nobody cared. Nobody really cared. He supposed he ought to stop his pacing, get out of his wet clothes, and then put a fifty-pence in the meter to run the electric fire. Otherwise, he'd catch his death of cold.

***

Arthur, back in his pyjamas and holey dressing gown, sat on the sofa finishing off a plate of baked beans on toast, with his bare feet pushed close enough to the electric fire for bodily warmth but far enough away so as not to turn his toes into ten lit matches. He'd decided to live it up, economising be damned, and turned on a full three bars of the electric fire. His only fifty-pence in the world wouldn't last long running the electric fire at its capacity while also running the single ceiling light bulb above his head, which illuminated the bedsit as though a séance was about to commence. He ate the last of his beans on toast and placed his knife and fork down on the plate. He'd made especially good baked beans on toast. Perhaps his best ever. As last meals went, not even a paneer tikka masala prepared by the Star of Bengal could've competed. Oh, how he remembered that takeaway! He'd treated himself the day he'd moved into the bedsit. He'd wanted to order the same after receiving his first paycheck. How ridiculous it had been for him to think he'd ever be lucky enough to order a second paneer tikka masala from the Star of Bengal! There were, however, always baked beans on toast sitting in front of an electric fire with three bars burning. That was, until a fifty-pence, that didn't go as far a fifty-pence used to go, decided enough warmth was enough warmth, and as for the light, well, that was enough light, too. Of course, and as if written in black notebook somewhere, there came a knock, knock, at the door.

If it happened after the first knock, or, for that matter, happened after the second knock, Arthur didn't know. It had happened, though. He no longer sat on the sofa in the dark and cold. He stood in the dark and cold, facing the door. What was he grasping? He looked down and saw it was a steak knife. The steak knife that came with the bedsit. His baked-beans-on-toast steak knife. What on earth was he thinking? What was he expecting of himself? He wasn't the fighting type. He was the getting-murdered type! He could very well use a steak knife for baked beans on toast, and expertly so, but he couldn't turn the same steak knife into a weapon. Could he? He'd have to practise. There came another knock, knock, at the door. Arthur tried a forward thrust with the steak knife. The steak knife dropped from his hand to the carpet. Had he heard laughter? He looked about as though to check there wasn't another person in the bedsit who'd witnessed his clumsiness. For a brief moment he thought he did see a person in the darkness, but the person quickly became Sunny's birdcage. The laughter had to have come from another tenant in the building. That person couldn't have known what he was up to, could they? It wasn't as though he was appearing on their TV. He bent over and picked up the steak knife. Obviously, the forward thrust was beyond his current knifing skills. He could try a hacking motion. That would be simple enough, up and down, up and down, like he was trying to extract a pickled onion from a glass jar. Once again, the steak knife fell from his hand. Once more, he picked up the steak knife. If he couldn't perform the forward thrust or the hack, what other attacking move was there? He'd committed himself to a slashing movement with the steak knife before he could stop himself. The steak knife flew from his grip and inserted itself point first into the door. A knock, knock at the same door was the response. Now the murderer knew he was at home, if they hadn't known already.

Arthur crept towards the door, not to answer his caller—Mildred had told him not to do that, whatever else he did—but to retrieve the steak knife. How was he supposed to butter his toast with his one and only knife embedded into the door? How was he supposed to eat his baked beans on toast? He'd fallen far in his life, but he wouldn't permit himself to sink so low as to not possess a usable knife to accompany his usable fork. On his way to the door, with the darkness upholstering the interior of his coffin-like bedsit with black satin, he stubbed his foot against the table chair. He stifled a cry of pain by placing both hands to his mouth while hopping up and down and about upon his undamaged foot. In so doing, he hopped backwards onto the empty dinner plate he'd put down onto the carpet, in particular hopping onto the tines of his usable fork. He quickly changed his hopping foot to the foot that now hurt a little less and off the foot that suddenly hurt a whole lot more. As for his hands, they remained firmly gaffer-taped to his mouth. Somewhere in the house, he heard the same laughter from the same tenant. On the other side of his door, he heard the same two knocks from the same murderer. Then, he heard a voice: "Is there anyone in? I heard someone in. I've got myself turned all the way up. Are you in?" The voice belonged to an old woman, he was sure of it. But it wasn't Ethel's or Mildred's voice. Could the murderer be an old woman? Surely not. He hobbled over to the door. He put an eye to the peephole. It was an old woman. She looked like the kind of old woman who knew how to knit. She didn't look like the kind of old woman who knew how to murder. "If you're in there," the old woman said, "I'm out here. I've been knocking. Knock, knock. That was me. Are you in?"

Arthur opened his door to the old woman, if for nothing else to encourage her to go away and leave him alone. Would she ever have stopped knocking on his door? He couldn't have every Tom, Dick, and Old Woman knocking at his door. There was a murderer to come calling, to come knocking, knock, knock. He couldn't cope with an inquiry other than the murderer's inquiry.

With the door finally open, the old woman looked relieved to see Arthur. "You're in. I knew you were in. Thank goodness you're in. I thought I'd have to knock, knock all the evening long and miss my show. I wouldn't have wanted that." She noticed Arthur's clothing. "Ready for bed, I see."

Arthur put a hand over the hole in his dressing gown. "Can I help you?"

"You can't help me," the old woman said. "I'm ninety-three in December. I'm past the point of helping. No, you can't help me. But I can help you. Now come closer. We'll be able to have a better chat with you closer. I've got myself turned all the way up, but I still have bother. I used to be able to hear for free. Now I can't afford the batteries." She fiddled around with her hearing aid. "Come on, closer, closer, I haven't got time to waste. My show's about to start. I never miss my show. It's the only thing that's keeping me alive. Forget the murderer. If I ever couldn't watch my show, that would be it for me: dead on the spot. Now are you going to come closer, or did I waste my time coming all the way up here?" She peered beyond Arthur into the darkness of his bedsit. "I know your room. Shaped like a bloody coffin. A bit gloomy in there, isn't it? Don't you want to see things? You'd be better off seeing things." She put her hands on her hips. "You haven't moved. You're still standing there. Can you move? What you got, glue on your feet? Closer, closer, I won't bite. My kettle would be boiled now for my cup of tea. I always have a cup of tea and a couple of jammie dodgers with my show. I once tried a coffee with a couple of ginger snaps, but it wasn't the same." She frowned and her face struggled mightily to accommodate the extra onslaught of wrinkles. "You haven't said anything either. You haven't moved. And you haven't said anything. Is it medication time for you? I get like you sometimes when I forget to take mine. Don't want to move. Don't want to speak. But I still watch my show with my cup of tea and jammie dodgers. Do you have something like that in your life? Something like my show? A bright spot in your day to keep you going, like? If you don't, there's always my show. Have you seen it? You should see it. Ooh, it's ever so good." She pointed at Arthur. "Here's an idea, why don't you come downstairs to mine and watch my show with me? We can talk about what I came up to talk to you about after. Not in my show, there'll no talking in my show. Come on, I've enough tea and jammie dodgers for two." She took Arthur by the arm and led him from out of his doorway. "That's it. You can move when you want to, can't you? One foot after the other, there you go. You're doing fine. We'll work on the talking later. One thing at a time, eh? Now, best the two of us get a move on if we're going to make our show. It's going to be another good one tonight. I read about it in the paper. Lots of drama. Then I read about the murderer. I didn't want to, but I did." She shook her head and tutted. "My Barry, he's always been a cross to bear, but then we all have those, don't we? You look like you've got ten crosses strapped to your back, mind you. I see people like you all the time. Then I don't. It's a shame. Nobody cares, do they? I do, but I'm ninety-three in

December. There's not much the likes of me can do for the likes of you. I'm doing my best, though. Now, don't go falling down the stairs. It's like Everest, isn't it? You go first. I'll follow with directions for you. When the lights go off, don't worry. My hearing may've packed up, but I can see like a bat in the dark." She laid a crumpled tissue paper hand upon Arthur's back. "Oh, my Big Barry! If he doesn't win his darts tonight, I don't need to tell you what might happen. Yes, god forbid him losing his darts. He's in the quarters, you know. He's very proud of himself for being in the quarters. Tells his mother most things he does. For the better or the worse. For the worse most of the time. Us mothers, we have crosses to bear. One or more of them, they're forever heavy."

As Arthur couldn't help himself opening the door, as he couldn't help himself listening to the old woman's mesmerising ramblings without answer, as he couldn't help himself being taken to watch a show on the TV with a cup of tea and two jammie dodgers, he couldn't help remembering the luck he'd passed onto the bus driver for his darts match with Big Barry.

***

The old woman's name was Margaret, but she'd told Arthur to call her Marge, which was appropriate, she'd said, as she was one of those strange ones who preferred the taste of margarine over the taste of butter. Tea drank and jammie dodgers eaten, Arthur sat next to Marge on a lumpy settee facing the TV, upon which the characters in Marge's show came and went saying and doing this and that—not that he'd being paying much attention to the show, not since he'd noticed the many framed photos of a person—the same person, he was sure of it—atop polished furniture and hung up on violet flock wallpapered walls. The photos spanned decades, and as he looked from one photo to another, he saw the person grow up before his eyes, through black and white and into colour, through boyhood and into manhood. However, at first, the photos had all seemed to be of rooms and landscapes, without a human subject photographed. Then, as Marge's TV show blared away, he slowly realised the wool had been pulled over his eyes. There was indeed a human subject within each and every one of the photos. Though rather than set in the photo's forefront, the boy, the man, was set back in the photo, blended into the room or landscape, part of the scenery, a person for finding and not for seeing. Unsettlingly, if his attention wandered away from the boy, the man, they would, seemingly, again be absent from the photo, and when his attention returned, they'd be there again, but only on looking and looking and looking. On looking, too, he saw that the boy, the man, always held a large sack, the kind of sack used for storing vegetables, the sack sometimes limp and at other times bulging.

"That's my Barry," Marge said, having switched off the TV, looking where Arthur was looking. "I see you see him. Few people see him. You have to look. Then you still might not see him. But I see you see my Barry. That's him all around us. Small Barry and Big Barry. But small or big, he'll always be my Barry to me."

Arthur wanted to know and didn't want to know, unseeing and then seeing, seeing and then unseeing, Marge's Barry, small and big. If he didn't ask, he'd regret not asking. "What's in the sacks?" he asked.

"Collections," Marge said. "Barry's always been a collector . It's his hobby. It's nice to have a hobby, don't you think? He's collected some things over the years. Oh my! Now, let me think. It was conkers in 1977. In 1983, it was my tears. In 1999, it was all sorts of metal. Barry collects whatever takes his fancy. You never know what it's going to be.

He never says what it's going to be. I've tried guessing, but I'm always wrong. I can guess ten-pence pieces and it ends up being dirt. That was in 2015. Just plain dirt to me, but special dirt to my Barry. Sack after sack of collections. He fills the sack up. And that's it for a collection. Time for a new one. You never know what it's going to be." She patted Arthur's knee. "That brings me to me why I came up to see you. Why I brought you down to mine. My Barry has a new collection going. I can't say I know what the collection is for sure. I never guess right. But maybe I'm right this time. I read the paper. Do you read the paper? It's all over the front page, every day. People are talking about it like that's all they can talk about. A terrible business, it is. Those poor people. My poor Barry. Whatever got into him is in him now. It won't leave him until his collection is complete. I know my Barry. He has to fill his sack. I've never seen him stop collecting what he wants to collect until he fills his sack. It took him sixteen months and twenty-three days to complete his collection of spiders. I didn't enjoy that collection one bit. His sack would move. No, spiders aren't for me. I can't say I enjoy thinking about his new collection, either. If I'm right about it. And I think I'm right. It's keeping me up at nights. It's getting so I can hardly enjoy my show. I can't be having that, not even for my Barry. I suppose I should talk to the police instead of you. But the police have had more than their fair chances of doing their job. And where are they at? Nowhere, that's where they're at. All these days gone by, all those poor people gone. Why should I give the police another chance when I can give it to you? That's what I thought. It might not be the right thinking, but that's my thinking." She pointed to the coffee table in front of them. "You see that photo of my Barry, the one next to the oranges? You'll have to keep on looking to see my Barry. But even not seeing my Barry, do you see something you know is there?"

Arthur looked at the silver-framed photo and there was a single bed placed in the same place that his single bed was placed, with a bed cover that was the same as his bed cover. There was a threadbare sofa placed in the same place that his threadbare sofa was placed, with the same sags and stains as his sofa's sags and stains. There was a bedsit room shaped like a coffin in the same way that his bedsit room was shaped like a coffin.

Marge sighed. "In them days, I knew where my Barry was. He was upstairs in yours. Nowadays, I don't know. I see like a bat, but my Barry has gotten harder to see. Even for me, and I'm his mother. Now I look and I might as well be looking to see what's down a plughole. My Barry always said he'd come home again. He didn't want to go. But Ethel and Mildred were having none of it. His collection of radios was too loud for the neighbours. It was stop your collection or go. What a palaver! Ethel wouldn't even paint his portrait. Well, my Barry didn't want to stop his collection. Once he starts, he doesn't stop. Not until his collection is complete. Now he's back home again. I know he is. I thought I saw him, but then I didn't see him. That's as good as seeing him in my book. I guess I should tell the police, but I'm telling you. My Barry's back home with his new collection. I heard him knocking the other night. The entire house must've heard. I knew it was my Barry. A mother knows these things. Knock, knock. Knock, knock. On your door. I thought I saw him and then I didn't see him. That's my Barry for you. His darts must be over by now. He never let people in his room. Knock, knock. Knock, knock. You know what the knocking sounded like to me? Didn't sound like my Barry's hand knocking to me. Oh, no. Sounded like a heavy sack knocking, knock, knock. Big and thunderous. Sounded like his collection was almost complete. He never let people into his room, not even his mother. I'd be going if I were you when my Barry's got a collection to complete. He'll be back home soon enough, my Barry. Knock, knock. Knock, knock. Who's there? My Barry, that's who. My Barry."

***

Arthur walked the cold and wet night streets carrying a suitcase in one hand and clutching a potted primrose to his chest with his other hand. He'd been walking a long time. He didn't know where he was going. He wasn't alone. There were other people walking the night streets, too. Here and there. Men. Women. Children. They looked a lot like him in their own way. At first, he didn't see them. Then he saw them. Then he didn't see them. He didn't think he'd ever seen such people before. They didn't appear to know where they were going, either. He really didn't want to see the people. He was glad when they disappeared. The people reminded him of himself. He wouldn't look anymore, thank you very much. He didn't want to be reminded of himself. Where could he go when he didn't know where he was going? If he kept on walking, perhaps there'd be a place for him to go, a place for him to be? He saw a woman with urgency in her stride. He shouldn't have been looking, but he saw. He heard her before he saw her. The woman's high heels click-clicked over the pavement. She looked familiar. She sounded familiar. Then she was gone. She was there and then she was gone. A magic trick. He felt like he was about to disappear, too. He had to find a place to go, a place to be before he disappeared. If he didn't, he'd disappear. He didn't want to disappear. Brian had found the crooked house. Brian had said he could join him in the crooked house. That would be somewhere to go, a place to be. Brian in the crooked house seemed a long way off. Was he still in the crooked house? Had he disappeared? How soon before he disappeared, like the woman in the high heels? Like the other people he didn't want to see, the people who reminded him of himself. They were there and then they were gone. Perhaps he'd already disappeared? Ethel and Mildred hadn't seen him leaving the house, and he'd walked past them down the driveway. They were looking his way as he was going their way and they didn't see him. They didn't say a word. Not a hello. Not a goodbye. They didn't seem to care. Had his magic trick already happened? Had it yet to happen? How soon before he turned a corner and thought himself not around the corner? Where would he end up? He turned a corner and, knock knock, he thought he found himself a grotesque portrait. A portrait of a man gone mad. A portrait of a man encountering his demise, eyes painted with fear spiralling, a mouth painted a black hole scream. He heard a chorus of: "Nobody cares. Nobody cares. Nobody cares." Where would all the other people he'd seen that evening end up when he and the others from the house, knock knock, had ended up where they were? He joined the chorus of voices.

End

Also by Daz Eek

Daz Eek is also the author of *The Crows That Ate Sunday*.

Join Daz Eek's newsletter for news on future book releases at https://dazeek.blog/.